Little Yau

A Fuzzhead Tale

JANELL CANNON

HARCOURT, INC.

San Diego   New York   London

Manufactured in China

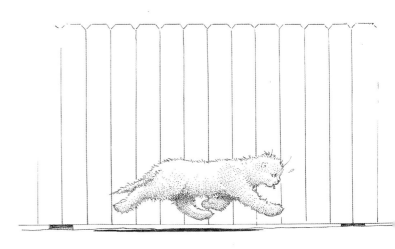

For Taita Pacho and all who learn from him

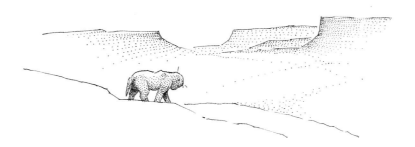

Today was the day of the big test. Little Yau had studied hard, collecting all the plants she needed to make Fever-gone, Nose-ease, and Open-ear.

I'll mix these herbs faster and better than any other apprentice Trau has known! she vowed. *Then the Wise Ones will invite me to the mountains to teach me the great secrets.* She trotted into the medicine cave, eager to begin.

Trau, her teacher, was waiting. "Please make a bowl of Ache-no-more," he said.

Little Yau gulped. "Ache-no-more?" she squeaked. *I studied everything except Ache-no-more!* She fumbled about, plucking at dried leaves and shuffling trays of bark and seeds. "One bowl of Ache-no-more, coming up!" she fibbed.

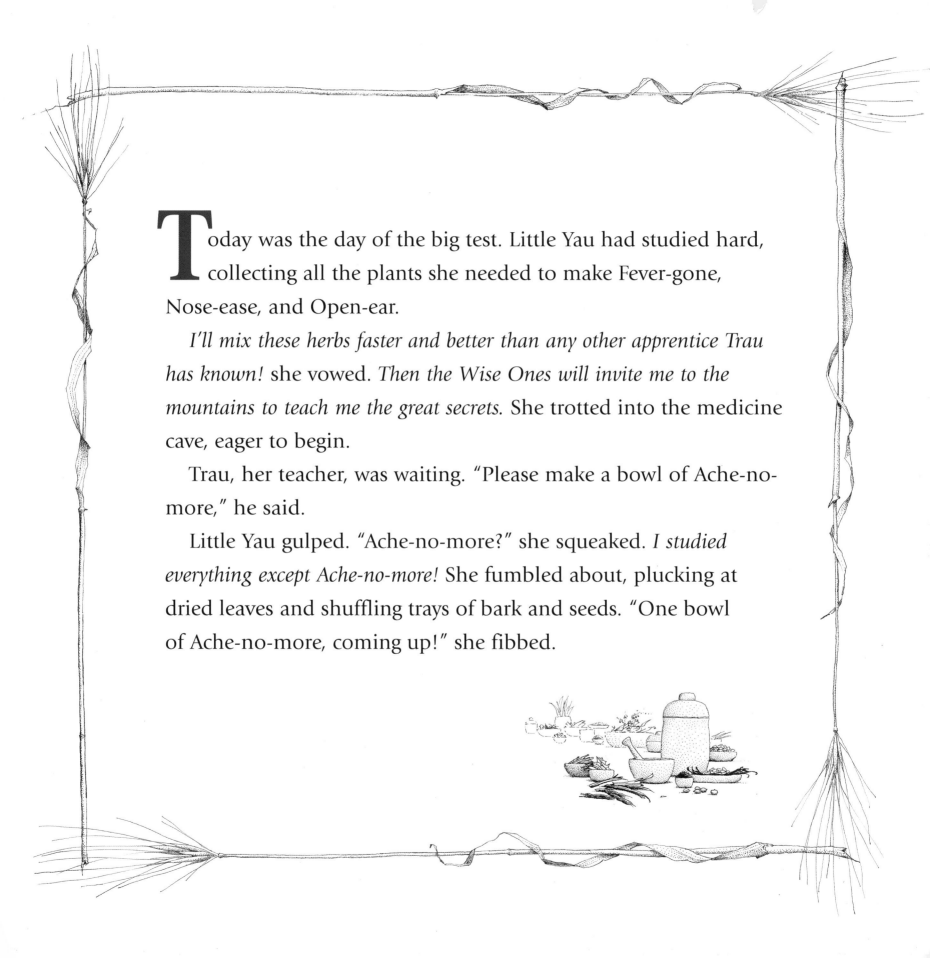

She hastily sprinkled this and that into the mixing bowl, then reached for the water pitcher. Her elbow knocked the bowl onto the stone floor, where it shattered into tiny pieces.

Trau frowned. "Stop," he ordered. "You are unprepared. One must not waste precious plants to save one's pride."

Little Yau crawled around, trying to sweep up the broken bowl. "I am very sorry," she gasped. She ran out of the medicine cave, her face hot with shame. *The Wise Ones will never take me to the mountains now!*

How she wished Trupp would come back! He had been gone for a very long time on a journey, and Little Yau missed him terribly. Today, like every day, she traveled down the steep, narrow path to the old riverbed, hoping to be the first to welcome her best friend home.

Climbing to the highest point, Little Yau scanned the red rock maze—and there was Trupp. He lay far below in the canyon, asleep on the warm boulders. Little Yau hopped from ledge to ledge and scrambled to his side.

"Welcome home!" she cheered. But Trupp didn't move. "Trupp? Wake up!" There were dark circles under his eyes. Little Yau raced faster than she had ever run in her life back to the medicine cave, calling for others to carry Trupp back to the village.

Mau and Trau reached Trupp in record time. Trau carefully looked him over and said, "He's not asleep—he's been poisoned." Mau gently gathered Trupp into his arms and ran back to the village on his hind legs.

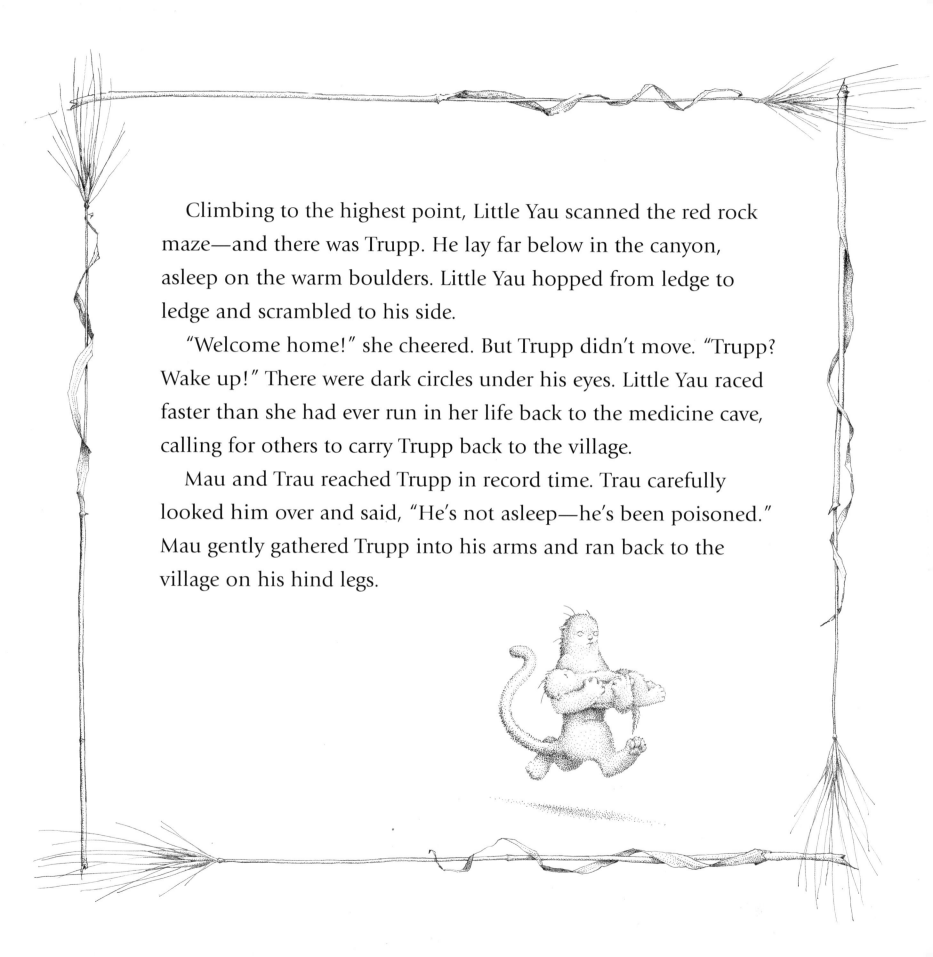

In minutes, everyone in the village gathered at the medicine cave. Trau covered Trupp with a healing quilt while he gave Little Yau directions. Her paws shook as she whipped up a bowl of Fever-gone. She felt lucky that she had studied that one. This was no time to fail again.

All was quiet as Trau slowly placed a few drops of the green syrup under Trupp's tongue. "This will help him fight the poison," Trau informed the others. A few began to hum a healing song. Soon all joined in, surrounding Trupp with a soft, comforting melody.

As afternoon light crept into the cave, Trupp wasn't getting better. Trau and Little Yau kept mixing, hoping they would find the right formula. But Trupp's nose had turned blue, and that was a very bad sign.

Trau leaned toward Yau and said quietly, "It's my turn to flunk now. We need help." Then he boldly announced, "We must call the elders. Mau! Rau! To the Great Arch!"

Rau and Mau followed Trau, and the three quickly scaled the Great Arch, the high place where their voices could be heard by the Wise Ones. They each took a deep breath and sang out a loud, continuous tone. Each sound was different, but they blended into a beautiful harmony that lifted through the darkening skies, over the red rock village, and up into the mountains.

Little Yau listened to the calling song. She loved the Wise Ones and was eager to see them. They so rarely came down from their mysterious forest world. *Somehow they always know what to do,* Yau marveled as she pulled the healing quilt up around Trupp.

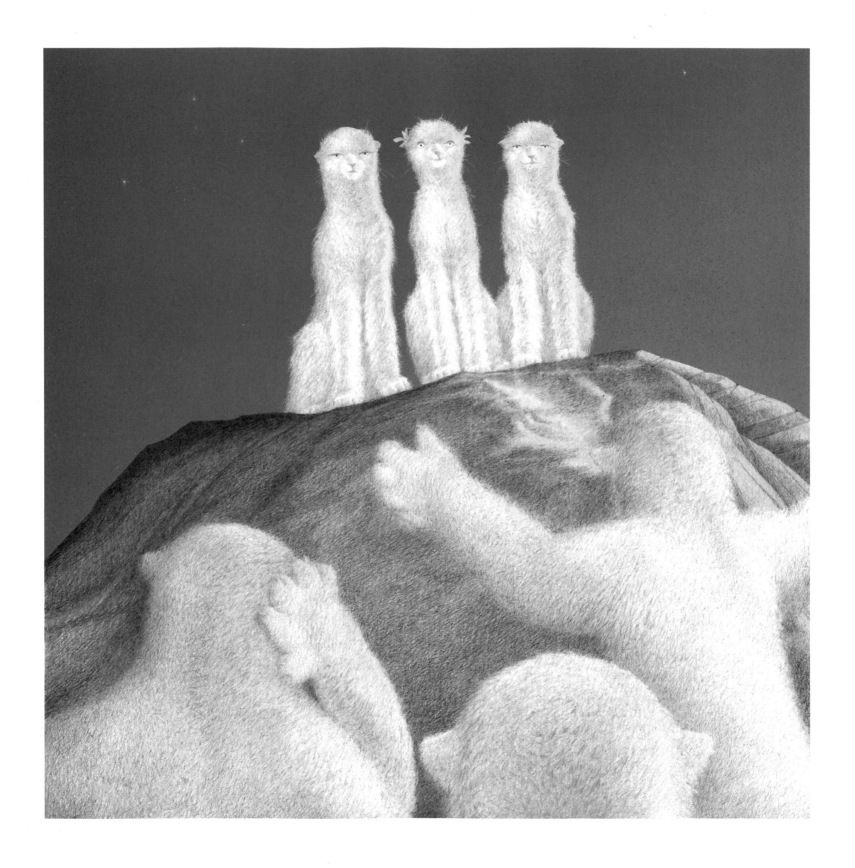

"What'll it be, kids?" said a gravelly voice.

Trau, Rau, and Mau jumped and nearly toppled off the Great Arch. "How do you *do* that?" they gasped, and ran to hug Rowl, Rup, and Eermp.

The Wise Ones were the oldest Fuzzheads of all. They were a bit scrawny and their coats were patchy, unlike the thick fur coats of the younger ones. They smelled like musty leaves on a forest floor. But none of the young ones cared. Eermp always wore sweet-scented plants behind each ear, and so she smelled the best.

"We must hurry!" urged Trau. "It's Trupp. He's been poisoned." They all rushed back to the medicine cave. Little Yau ran out to meet them and pulled them inside.

"Let's take a look," said Eermp as the Wise Ones gathered closely around their young patient.

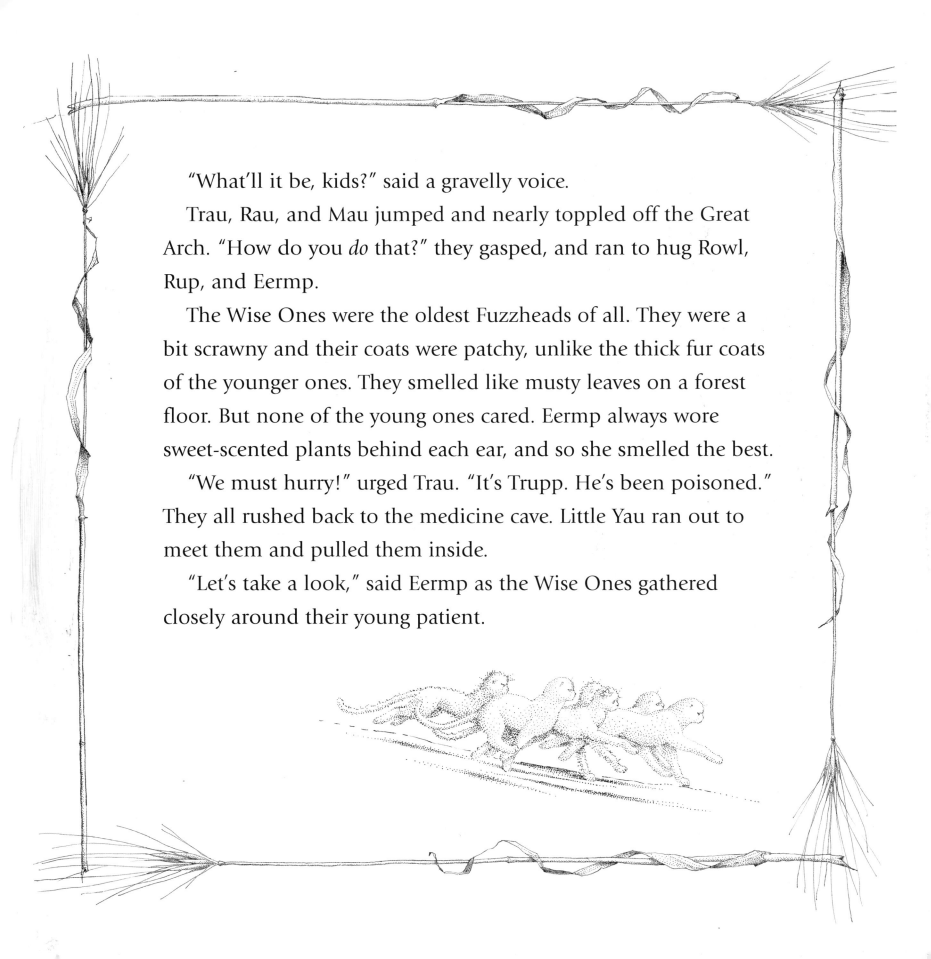

"Hmmm. This seems familiar," whispered Rowl. He was the oldest and had seen the most. He gazed into the little one's face and carefully touched Trupp's blue nose. Then he buried his face in Trupp's furry forehead, took a deep breath, and jumped back, sneezing violently.

Blinking through teary eyes, he said, "I remember now. It's poison from the human garden. The last time this happened we used thumbfoot leaf as a cure. It's a vine that has a footprint pattern on its leaves. It's very rare and hard to find."

"I've seen it before!" Little Yau burst out, trying not to jump around like a foolish cub. "I know where it is!"

"Lead the way." Rowl waved his paw toward the cave door, then looked at Trau and said, "You must bathe him immediately. We will return soon."

Little Yau streaked out of the cave, and she and the Wise Ones vanished into the night. On the dark trail, the healing song in the village grew faint. So as she ran, Yau began to hum the song herself.

"I *swear* this is the place!" howled Little Yau.

"They covered it!" groaned Eermp. "Whatever's left of the thumbfoot plant is under this smooth, black rock."

Yau threw herself down, clawing at the hard surface. "It's here—I *know* it is!" she wailed.

Rowl swept her up into his arms and sighed. "We have to keep looking."

"But where?" asked Eermp.

"*Everywhere!*" said Rowl. "We'll search day and night. You saw that blue nose—there isn't much time."

"It's dangerous here. There are too many humans around," said Rup. "We must find human clothes to disguise ourselves."

"How about that human village we passed on the way here?" suggested Eermp.

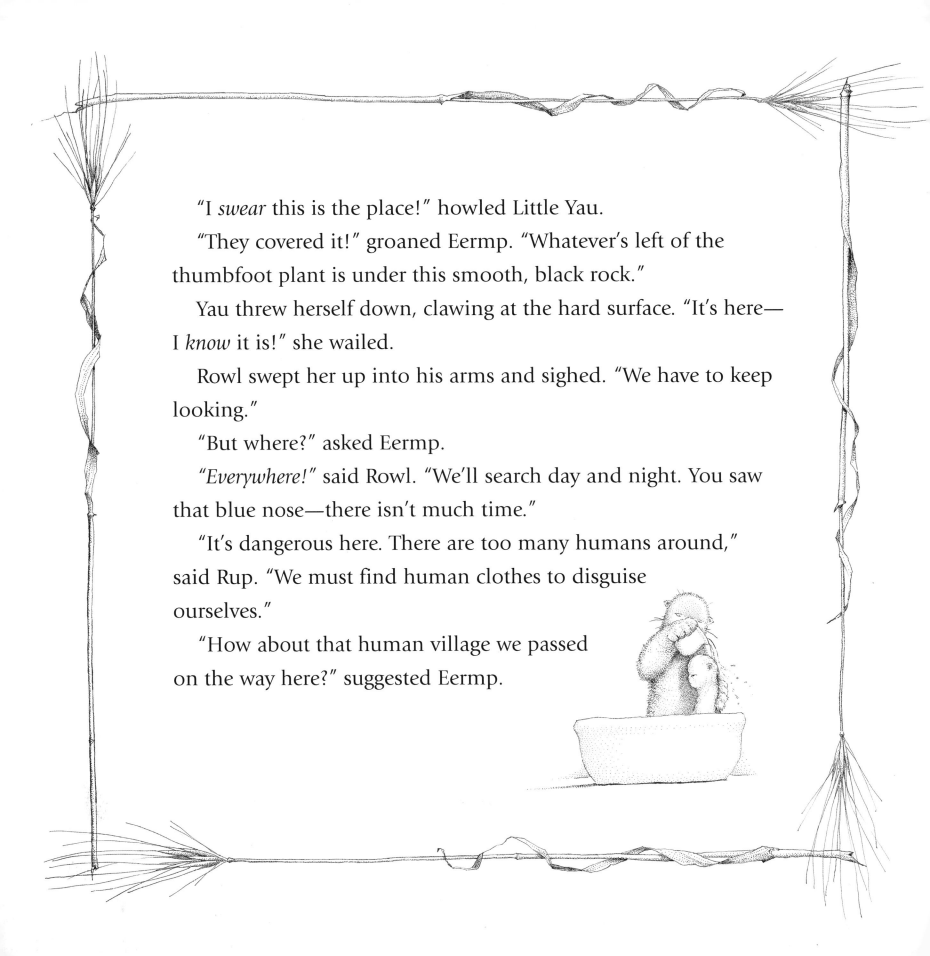

They set off. Yau had never run so fast or so far in her life, and soon her ribs hurt. Just when she thought she couldn't go any further, they reached the village.

"Why are human paths so smooth and flat? Is that a glass window? That's a car, right?" Little Yau babbled. "Are there plants buried under this village?"

"Shh!" Eermp hushed. Then she whispered, "Because they trip easily. Yes, yes, and probably."

They moved silently near the buildings, pacing up and down each street.

"Look!" Rup said. "I can't believe what I see!"

There, under a dim light, was a table piled with clothes in front of a darkened Laundromat. They darted over, grabbing whatever was nearest.

Hiding in an alley, they struggled into their disguises.

"I don't know how people can stand to wear this stuff!" Eermp grunted as she dressed. Rup hopped around on one leg, trying to pull up his pants. Little Yau had never worn human clothes before, and Rowl helped her tug a shirt over her head.

"We have to go separate ways," said Rowl. "And we've got to move fast—but remember to stay on your hind legs! We're supposed to be humans now." Then he turned to Yau. "We will let you search alone—but you must be very careful."

"And try not to talk!" said Eermp. "I trust you have studied the Human Phrase Book. Use that if you get stuck."

"Easy-as-pie," said Little Yau.

"I hope we find the thumbfoot soon," Rup hissed. "These boots are killing my feet!"

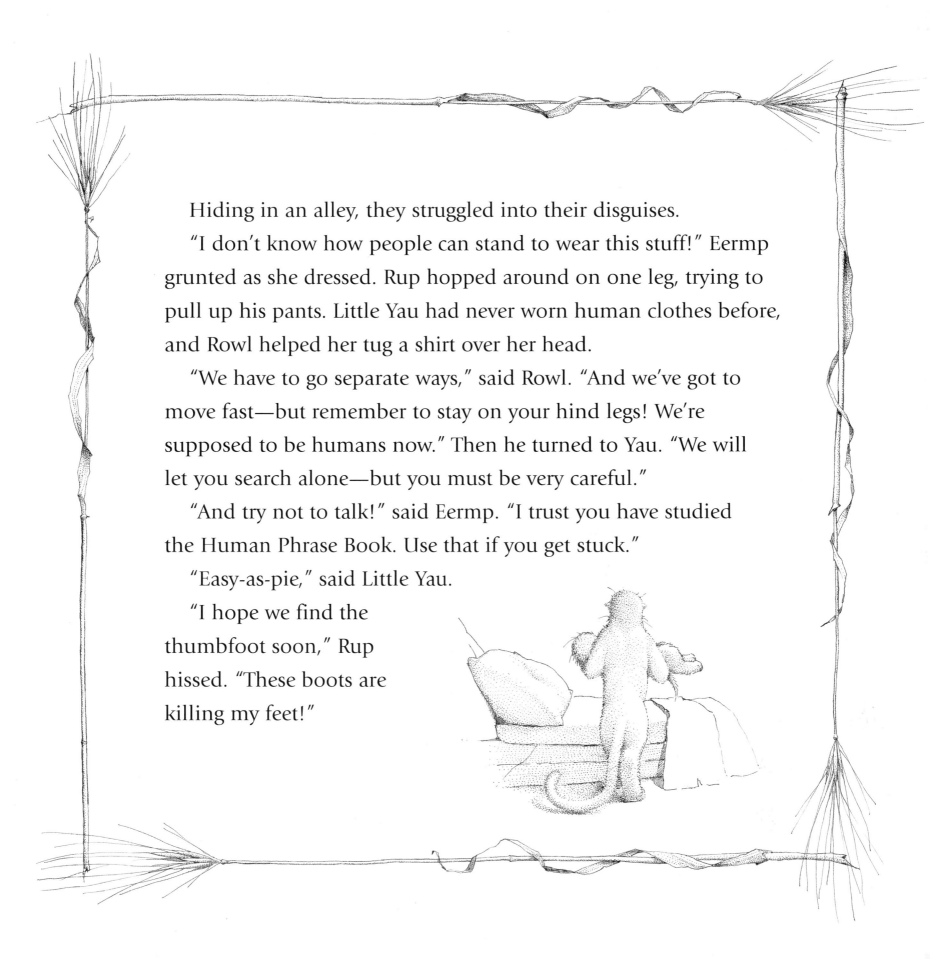

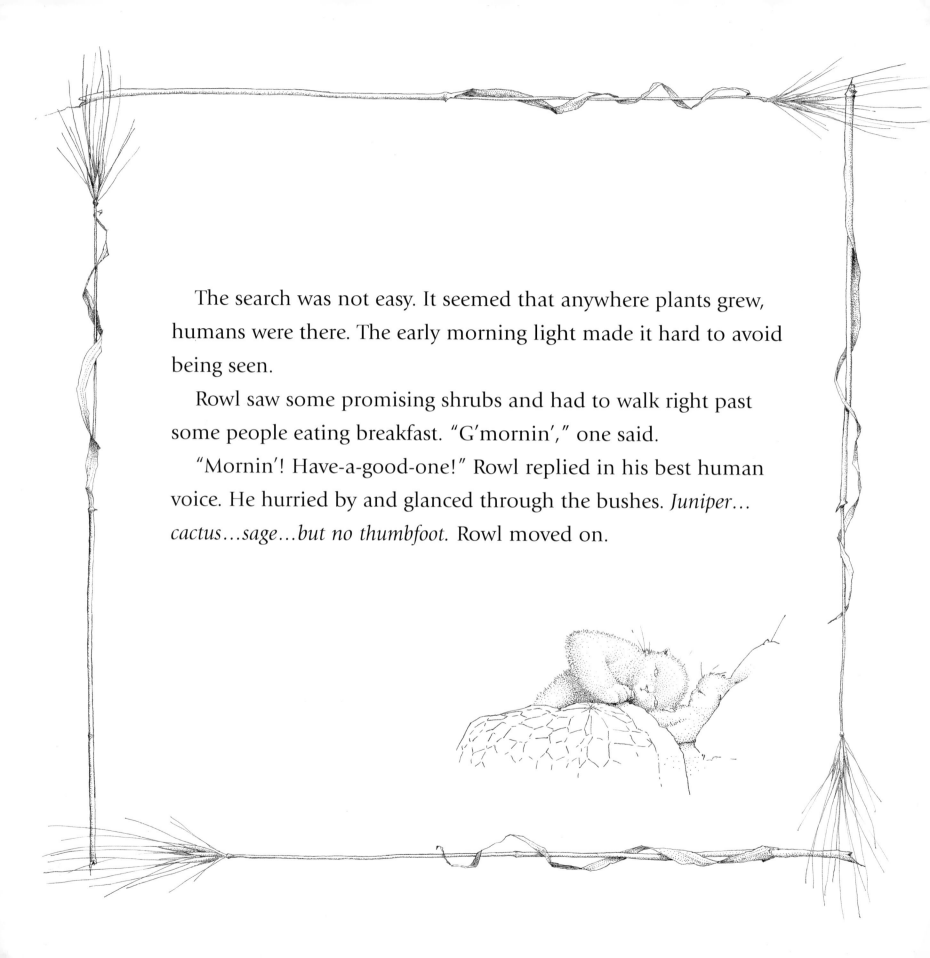

The search was not easy. It seemed that anywhere plants grew, humans were there. The early morning light made it hard to avoid being seen.

Rowl saw some promising shrubs and had to walk right past some people eating breakfast. "G'mornin'," one said.

"Mornin'! Have-a-good-one!" Rowl replied in his best human voice. He hurried by and glanced through the bushes. *Juniper… cactus…sage…but no thumbfoot.* Rowl moved on.

Eermp ducked into a canyon. She crept about on all fours, clawing through the thick bushes.

A loud rustling startled her—then a gigantic dog burst through the thicket, barking and snarling. Eermp froze.

"LOBO! Get back here, you lummox!" a man yelled. Lobo stayed put, barking wildly. "Oh, sorry, ma'am. He isn't normally like this," the man said apologetically.

"No-problemo!" chirped Eermp, trying to sound natural. The man grabbed the dog by the collar and dragged him away.

Eermp frantically kept up her search.

It has to be here somewhere!

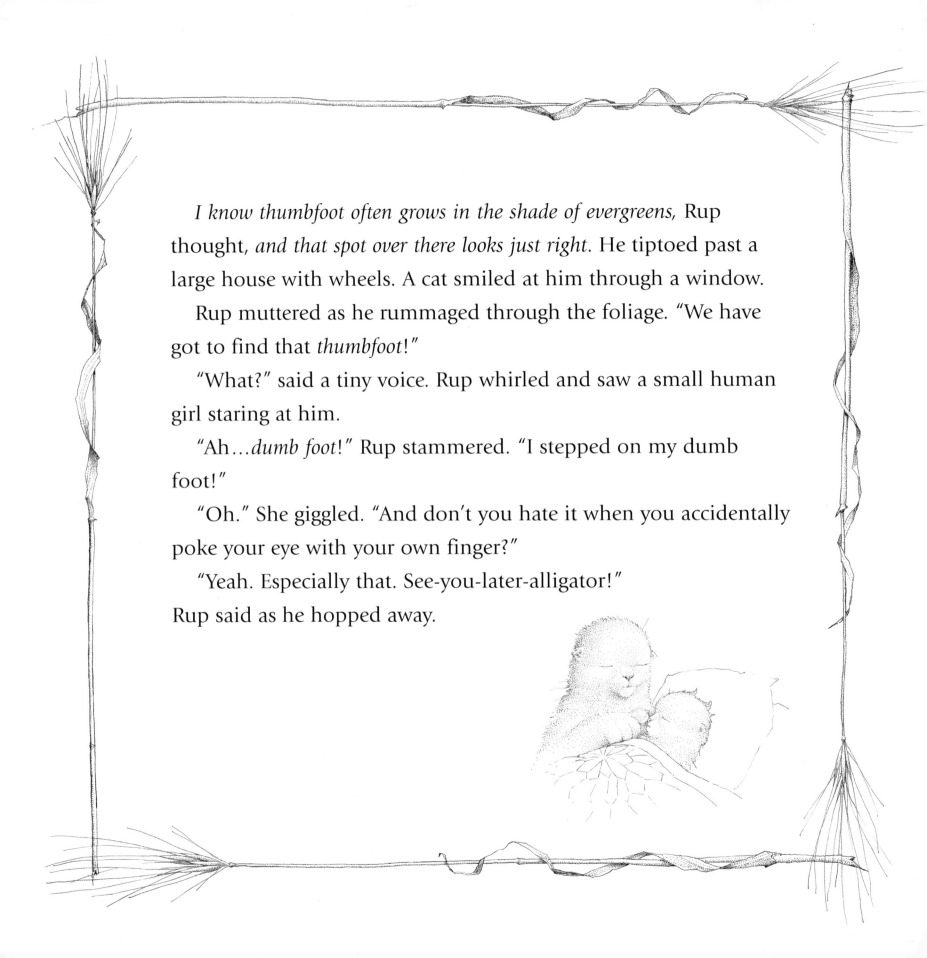

I know thumbfoot often grows in the shade of evergreens, Rup thought, *and that spot over there looks just right.* He tiptoed past a large house with wheels. A cat smiled at him through a window.

Rup muttered as he rummaged through the foliage. "We have got to find that *thumbfoot*!"

"What?" said a tiny voice. Rup whirled and saw a small human girl staring at him.

"Ah…*dumb foot*!" Rup stammered. "I stepped on my dumb foot!"

"Oh." She giggled. "And don't you hate it when you accidentally poke your eye with your own finger?"

"Yeah. Especially that. See-you-later-alligator!" Rup said as he hopped away.

Little Yau looked out over the land dotted with bright human dwellings. They looked like little caves made of colorful, floppy material.

The Wise Ones are counting on me to find thumbfoot, but I see nothing except human villages. All Yau could do was worry about Trupp. She softly hummed the healing song. A cool wind blew, and Little Yau's nose twitched. She thought she smelled the bitter scent of thumbfoot, and followed her nose. She had to walk near the humans to stay on track.

"Hello, dearie." A voice came from a blue cave. "Looking for your mom?"

"No. I-am-just-fine-and-dandy," replied Little Yau as she hurried by. She was glad that she had studied the tattered old Human Phrase Book Trau had given her.

Little Yau nervously searched the human village, her nose telling her that a thumbfoot plant was very near. Then—finally—she saw it.

The plant's leaves stuck out from the edge of an orange floppy cave. Most of it was flattened, but it was still alive. As quietly as she could, Little Yau sneaked up to the cave and quickly dug up the squashed thumbfoot, roots and all. With trembling paws, she put it in her backpack and ran full speed toward home, not even wondering where the Wise Ones were.

"Hang on, Trupp. We have thumbfoot!" Little Yau panted as she burst into the medicine cave. Eermp, Rup, and Rowl followed; they always knew where they were needed.

Little Yau unpacked the plant, plopped it in a pot, and added water. Rowl and Trau went immediately to work, cutting leaves and mixing them into a bowl of rain. Little Yau watched closely, memorizing Rowl's thumbfoot cure.

Eermp gently propped Trupp up in her lap. Even his tongue was blue now. "This will taste just hideous, but you'll feel better in a snap," Eermp whispered in his ear. Trau gently put a few drops of the thumbfoot brew into Trupp's mouth.

Everyone watched and waited…and waited…and waited.

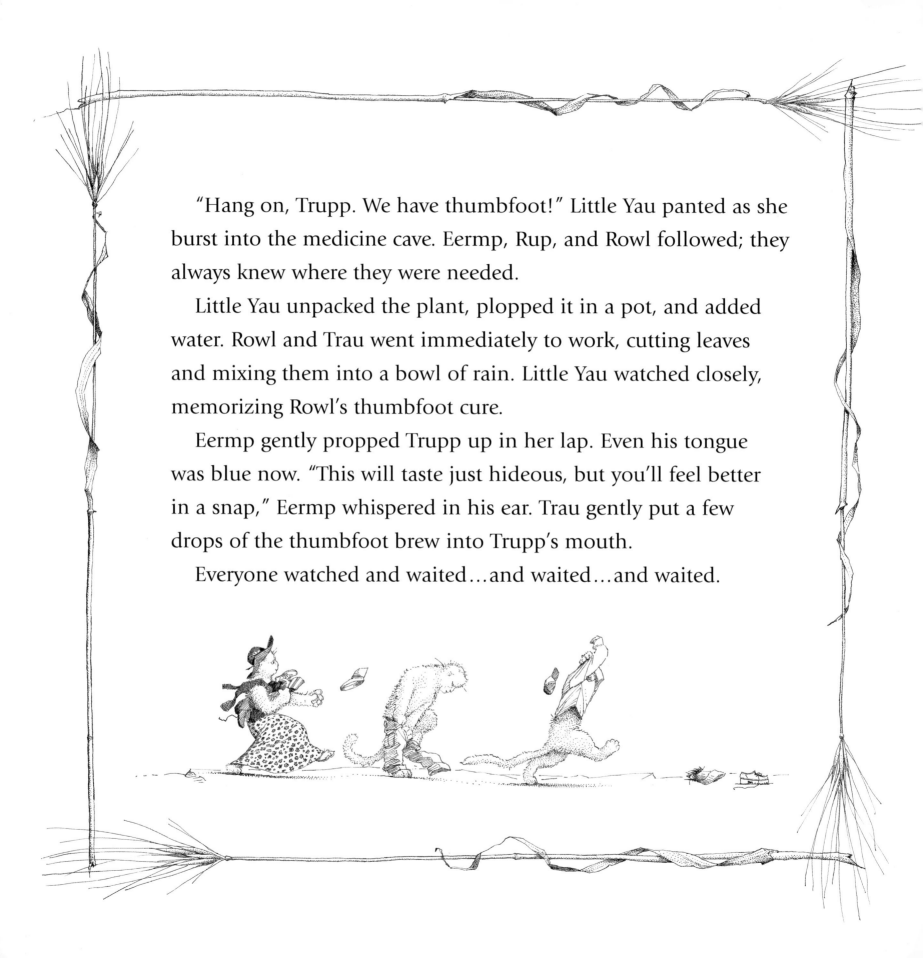

"His eyes are moving!" whispered Little Yau. She looked closer. "Now they're *open*!" she yelled, and spun about the cave, dancing with glee.

"And his nose is turning pink!" said Mau.

Eermp rocked Trupp's stirring body. "He's going to be all right," she purred.

Little Yau whirled and twirled like a tiny tornado. She danced as the healing song soared into a song of joy. Trupp's bleary eyes caught sight of his wild little friend and he laughed softly before he drifted off to sleep.

The next day, as the Wise Ones prepared to go home to the mountains, the whole village came out to say good-bye. Little Yau helped Trupp wobble out of the medicine cave. The elders each gave Trupp a lick on the top of the head with their dry old tongues.

"Take this and plant it nearby," Rup said as he gently handed Trupp the thumbfoot plant. "We will require this more than ever, and we can't be going on a panicked hunt whenever we are in need."

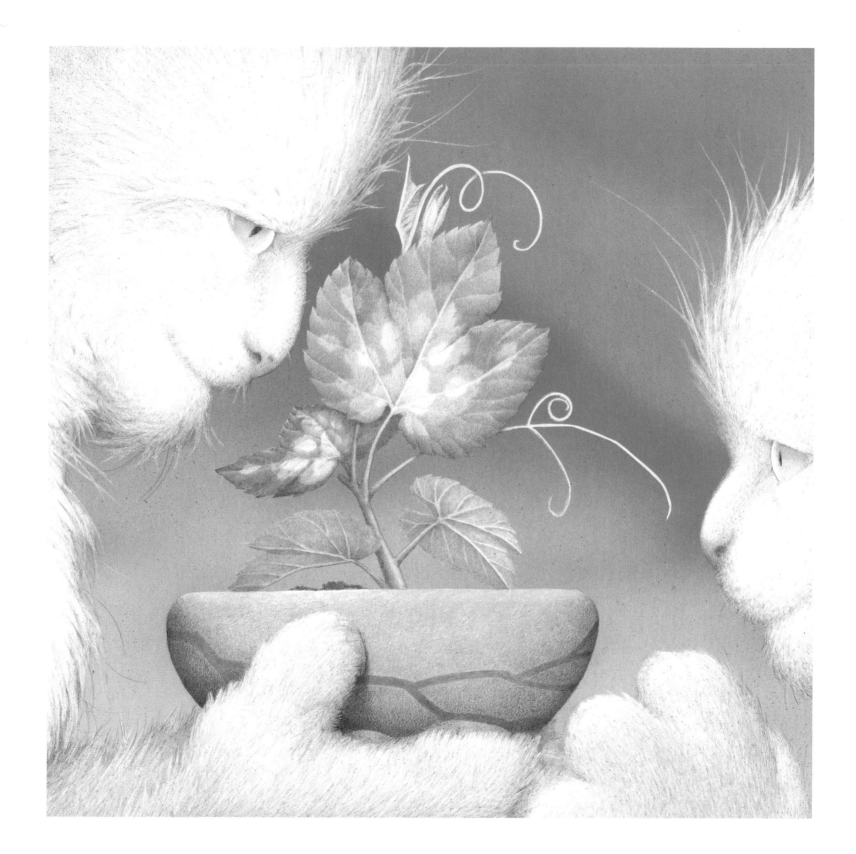

And then Rowl said something that made Yau and Trupp stare at him in shock. "Little Yau. We think you are ready to come with us to the mountains."

Little Yau glanced at Trupp and asked, "I am? But—but—but I need to help Trupp."

"Trupp needs to stay here and recover, and start the thumbfoot garden. Trau will take very good care of him," said Eermp. "You have a whole forest of new plants to meet."

Little Yau rushed to Trupp, wrapping her arms tightly around him. "Will I ever come back?"

"When the desert flowers bloom," answered Eermp. That sounded like a very long time to Little Yau, and she held her friend even tighter.

The Wise Ones touched foreheads with the others and gracefully loped off toward the mountains. They were not fond of long good-byes.

"When the elders ask you to go, you *go*," whispered Trupp. "They won't ask again."

Little Yau loosened her grip and gazed at him. "When the flowers bloom, I'll be back!" she said. "I promise!"

Then Little Yau ran after the Wise Ones, ready to follow her wildest dreams.

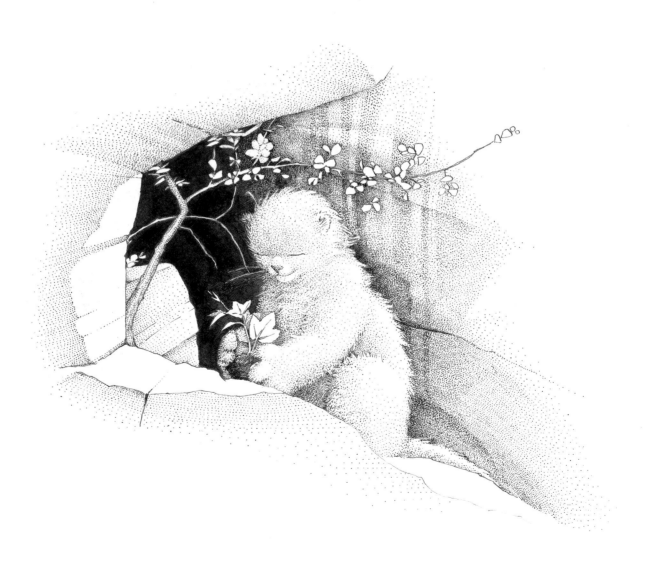

FUZZHEAD

(Blancofelis dexterodactylus)

Average adult weight: 200 pounds   Average adult height: 6 feet (standing)

These catlike creatures have a dense coat of soft white fur and crystalline blue eyes. Their front feet (or hands) have opposable thumbs, which allow dexterous handling of tools. Although omnivorous, they subsist primarily on fruits and vegetables.

The Fuzzhead population is estimated to be quite small. Counts are not accurate because these beings are highly secretive and often avoid human contact. Their life spans are thought to be as long as two hundred years.

Highly adaptable to a wide range of climatic and geographic conditions, Fuzzheads live on every continent in the world. They are exceptionally intelligent and have great talent in the art of healing with plants.

Fuzzheads love language, books, and libraries. They visit libraries and bookstores as often as they dare, always disguised in human clothes.

Peaceful and nonconfrontational, Fuzzheads have lived harmoniously through the millennia, hidden from humans, sharing their caves with any animal that needs shelter.

Thanks go to Jeannette Larson and Deborah Halverson for providing the ever-important editorial Objective Eye,
and to Judythe Sieck for her most dependable sense of color and design.

Requests for permission to make copies of any part of the work should be mailed to the following address:
Permissions Department, Harcourt, Inc., 6277 Sea Harbor Drive, Orlando, Florida 32887-6777.

www.HarcourtBooks.com

Library of Congress Cataloging-in-Publication Data
Cannon, Janell, 1957–
Little Yau: a Fuzzhead tale/Janell Cannon.
p.   cm.
Summary: When Trupp is poisoned, Little Yau and some of the other Fuzzheads don clothes and shoes
and venture into the world of humans, searching for the herb they need to make a cure.
[1. Herbs—Fiction.   2. Disguise—Fiction.]   I. Title.
PZ7.C1725Li   2002
[E]—dc21   2001006069
ISBN 0-15-201791-7

First edition

A C E G H F D B

The illustrations in this book were done in Liquitex acrylics and Prismacolor pencils on bristol board.
The display lettering was created by Judythe Sieck.
The text type was set in Giovanni Book.
Color separations by Bright Arts Ltd., Hong Kong
Manufactured by South China Printing Company, Ltd., China
This book was printed on totally chlorine-free Nymolla Matte Art paper.
Production supervision by Sandra Grebenar and Ginger Boyer
Designed by Judythe Sieck